Green Line 5

Vokabellernheft

herausgegeben von
Harald Weisshaar

Paul

Ernst Klett Verlag
Stuttgart · Leipzig

Vorwort

Liebe Schülerin, lieber Schüler,

in den vergangenen vier Schuljahren hast du eine ganze Menge Vokabeln gelernt und dir so schon einen beachtlichen englischen Wortschatz angeeignet. Das Green Line 5 Vokabellernheft unterstützt dich dabei, diesen im 9. Schuljahr noch zu erweitern. Du kannst mit dem Vokabellernheft den gesamten Lernwortschatz wiederholen und üben, und das nicht nur zu Hause, sondern auch unterwegs, denn es passt in die Hosentasche. Durch die Gliederung der Vokabeln nach den Buchteilen verlierst du nie den Überblick darüber, welche Wörter du schon kannst und welche du noch üben musst. Tipps zum Vokabellernen findest du zu Beginn jeder Unit.

Zusätzlich zum Wortschatz bietet dir dein Vokabellernheft auch abwechslungsreiche Übungen, in denen du die gelernten Wörter direkt nach jedem Abschnitt anwendest. Dies hilft dir dabei, die Vokabeln gut zu behalten, und bereitet dich gleichzeitig auf Tests vor. Am Ende jeder Unit bzw. Text smart gibt es eine Übung zur Selbstkontrolle (Check on your …), mit der du herausfinden kannst, wie fit du in einem bestimmten Thema bist.

Markiere beim Lernen alle Wörter und Wendungen, die du dir nicht so gut merken kannst, mit einem Bleistift. Wiederhole sie dann in regelmäßigen Abständen.

Mit den Lösungen auf den Seiten 73 bis 79 überprüfst du dich schließlich selbst.

Viel Spaß und Erfolg mit deinem Vokabellernheft!

Dein Green Line Team

Englische Laute

Mitlaute (Konsonanten)

[b]	**b**ed	[p]	**p**icture
[d]	**d**ay	[r]	**r**ed
[ð]	**th**e	[s]	**s**ix
[f]	**f**amily	[ʃ]	**sh**e
[g]	**g**o	[t]	**t**en
[ŋ]	morni**ng**	[tʃ]	**ch**air
[h]	**h**ouse	[v]	**v**ideo
[j]	**y**ou	[w]	**w**e, **o**ne
[k]	**c**an, mil**k**	[z]	ea**s**y
[l]	**l**etter	[ʒ]	revi**si**on
[m]	**m**an	[dʒ]	pa**ge**
[n]	**n**o	[θ]	**th**ank you

Selbstlaute (Vokale)

[ɑː]	c**a**r	[i]	happ**y**
[æ]	**a**pple	[iː]	t**ea**cher
[e]	p**e**n	[ɒ]	d**o**g
[ə]	**a**gain	[ɔː]	b**a**ll
[ɜː]	g**i**rl	[ʊ]	b**oo**k
[ʌ]	b**u**t	[u]	Jan**u**ary
[ɪ]	**i**t	[uː]	t**oo**, tw**o**

Doppellaute

[aɪ]	**I**, m**y**	[ɪə]	h**ere**, id**ea**
[aʊ]	n**ow**, m**ou**se	[əʊ]	hell**o**
[eɪ]	n**a**me, th**ey**	[ɔɪ]	b**oy**
[eə]	th**ere**, p**air**	[ʊə]	s**ure**

[ː] der vorangehende Laut ist lang, z. B. *you* [juː]

[‿] der Bindebogen zeigt, dass zwei Wörter in der Aussprache verbunden werden

[ˈ] die folgende Silbe trägt den Hauptakzent

[ˌ] die folgende Silbe trägt den Nebenakzent

Across cultures 1 The world speaks English

Tip

Da sich dein Englischwortschatz auch in diesem Schuljahr kontinuierlich erweitern wird, nimm dir zunächst die Zeit zu überlegen, welche Methoden dir in den letzten Jahren beim Vokabellernen tatsächlich geholfen haben. Sind es deine eigenen Vokabellisten, das Anlegen eines *personal vocabulary* zu den Hauptthemen der Units oder das Erstellen von Mindmaps zu bestimmten Wortfeldern? Lernst du lieber alleine oder hilft es dir, wenn dich jemand abhört? „Deine“ bewährte Methode wird dir später auch helfen, mit dem komplexeren Wortschatz in der Oberstufe zurechtzukommen.

square [skweə]	Quadrat; Quadrat-
including [ɪn'klu:dɪŋ]	einschließlich; inklusive
parliament ['pɑ:ləmənt]	Parlament
court [kɔ:t]	Hof; Gericht; Gerichtshof
racial ['reɪʃl]	Rassen-
segregation [ˌsegrɪ'geɪʃn]	Segregation; Trennung; Rassentrennung
bitterness *(no pl)* ['bɪtənəs]	Bitterkeit; Verbitterung
racism ['reɪsɪzm]	Rassismus
icon ['aɪkɒn]	Ikone; Symbol
civil rights *(pl)* [ˌsɪvl 'raɪts]	Bürgerrechte
election [ɪ'lekʃn]	Wahl
back [bæk]	damals
middle class [ˌmɪdl 'klɑ:s]	Mittelschicht
Hindu ['hɪndu:]	Hindu; hinduistisch
Muslim ['mʊzlɪm]	Muslim/-in; muslimisch
plastic surgery *(no pl)* [ˌplæstɪk 'sɜ:dʒəri]	Schönheitschirurgie

ancient ['eɪnʃnt]	alt; altertümlich; antik
spirituality [ˌspɪrɪtʃu'æləti]	Spiritualität
Buddhist ['bʊdɪst]	buddhistisch
romantic [rə'mæntɪk]	romantisch
mixed [mɪkst]	gemischt
reality [ri'æləti]	Realität; Wirklichkeit
democracy [dɪ'mɒkrəsi]	Demokratie
discrimination [dɪˌskrɪmɪ'neɪʃn]	Diskriminierung
widespread ['waɪdspred]	weit verbreitet
sexual ['sekʃʊəl]	sexuell
harassment [hə'ræsmənt]	Belästigung; Schikane
democratic [ˌdemə'krætɪk]	demokratisch
human rights [ˌhju:mən 'raɪts]	Menschenrechte
intense [ɪn'tens]	intensiv; heftig
I can't help *(+ -ing)* [aɪ ˌkɑ:nt 'help]	Ich kann nicht anders (als zu) …
to **turn on** [ˌtɜ:n‿'ɒn]	einschalten
chaotic [keɪ'ɒtɪk]	chaotisch
Latin ['lætɪn]	Latein; lateinisch
southern ['sʌðən]	südlich; Süd-
Italian [ɪ'tæliən]	Italiener/-in; italienisch; Italienisch; aus Italien
Chinese [tʃaɪ'ni:z]	Chinese/Chinesin; chinesisch; Chinesisch; aus China
Aboriginal [ˌæbə'rɪdʒnl]	von australischen Ureinwohnern abstammend
crocodile ['krɒkədaɪl]	Krokodil
saltie *(coll)* ['sɔ:lti]	Salzwasserkrokodil
length [leŋθ]	Länge
Aussie *(coll)* ['ɒzi]	Australier/-in; australisch *(ugs.)*
surf instructor [ˌsɜ:f‿ɪn'strʌktə]	Surflehrer/-in
to **envy** ['envi]	beneiden

to **apply (to)** [ə'plaɪ tə]	gelten (für); zutreffen (auf)
to **respect** [rɪ'spekt]	respektieren
resident ['rezɪdnt]	Bewohner/-in; Einwohner/-in
gay [geɪ]	schwul; homosexuell; Schwuler; Homosexueller
mate [meɪt]	Kumpel
to **head out** [ˌhed‿'aʊt]	hinausgehen
the outback [ði 'aʊtbæk]	Outback *(australisches Hinterland)*
bushfire ['bʊʃfaɪə]	Buschfeuer

1 Word pairs: The world speaks English

Make ten pairs of words and write them down.

human middle free ancient racial plastic civil surf square sexual

surgery culture harassment elections rights kilometre class segregation rights instructor

1. ______________________
2. ______________________
3. ______________________
4. ______________________
5. ______________________
6. ______________________
7. ______________________
8. ______________________
9. ______________________
10. ______________________

2 A closer look: Three English-speaking countries

Put in the missing words.

South Africa

1. In the 20th century, many black people suffered during the time of apartheid, a system of ______________________.
2. This system ended when ______________________ leader Nelson Mandela became South Africa's first president in free ______________________ in 1994.
3. Today there is a growing black ______________________.

India

1. Most people in India are ______________________, while some are ______________________ or practise other religions.
2. A lot of people from Western countries come to India to enjoy the ______________________ culture.
3. They call India 'the world's largest ______________________', but there are still problems with child labour and the ______________________ of women.

Australia

1. The name 'Australia' comes from the ______________ word 'australis', meaning '______________'.
2. Most Australians have a British or Irish background, but only 2.5% are ______________ Australians.
3. Australia offers an amazing wildlife. The world's largest ______________, Australia's 'salties', can grow to ______________ of six metres.

3 Word families: Nouns and adjectives

Complete the grid with the correct nouns or adjectives.

Nouns	Adjectives
	long
China	
	democratic
	real
chaos	
	racial

Unit 1 G'day Australia!

Tip

Wolltest du schon immer mehr über Australien wissen? Dann recherchiere im Internet englischsprachige Artikel über Australien. Dabei wirst du auch viele hilfreiche Wörter und Redewendungen finden, die dir bei der Arbeit mit der Unit weiterhelfen.

G'day! *(= Good day!)* [gə'daɪ]	Guten Tag.; Hallo.; Hi. *(Begrüßung in Australien)*

Station 1: Just me and my backpack

youth hostel ['ju:θ ˌhɒstl]	Jugendherberge
to **gleam** [gli:m]	glänzen; schimmern
cluster ['klʌstə]	Bündel; Anhäufung
giant [dʒaɪənt]	Riesen-; riesig
seashell ['si:ʃel]	Muschel
to **overhear** [ˌəʊvə'hɪə], **overheard** [ˌəʊvə'hɜ:d], **overheard** [ˌəʊvə'hɜ:d]	belauschen; zufällig mit anhören
owner ['əʊnə]	Besitzer/-in
terrace ['terɪs]	Terrasse
snake [sneɪk]	Schlange
air ambulance ['eər‿æmbjələns]	Rettungshubschrauber
satellite ['sætlaɪt]	Satellit
to **go off** [gəʊ‿'ɒf]	weggehen
on one's own [ˌɒn wʌnz‿'əʊn]	allein; für sich
bushwalking ['bʊʃˌwɔ:kɪŋ]	Buschwandern
box jellyfish ['bɒks ˌdʒelifɪʃ]	Würfelqualle
marine stinger [məˌri:n 'stɪŋə]	Seewespe *(Würfelquallen-Art)*

to **net off** [net‿'ɒf]	durch ein Netz abtrennen
to **be likely** [bi 'laɪkli]	wahrscheinlich sein
rip current ['rɪp ˌkʌrnt]	Brandungsrückströmung
to **be swept out to sea** [bi ˌswept‿aʊt tə 'si:]	aufs offene Meer getrieben werden
comforting ['kʌmfətɪŋ]	tröstlich; ermutigend
safety ['seɪfti]	Sicherheit
to **call off** [ˌkɔ:l‿'ɒf]	abbrechen; absagen
risk [rɪsk]	Gefahr; Risiko
spokesperson ['spəʊksˌpɜ:sn]	Sprecher/-in; PR-Sprecher/-in
association [əˌsəʊʃi'eɪʃn]	Verband; Organisation
survival [sə'vaɪvl]	Überleben
climatic [klaɪ'mætɪk]	klimatisch
mostly ['məʊstli]	meistens; größtenteils; hauptsächlich
interior [ɪn'tɪəriə]	Inneres; Landesinneres
to **show sb around (a place)** [ˌʃəʊ‿ə'raʊnd]	jmdn. (an einem Ort) herumführen
barbie *(infml)* **(= barbecue)** ['bɑ:bi]	Grillparty
to **serve** [sɜ:v]	servieren; dienen; bedienen
to **pick** [pɪk]	pflücken
litter ['lɪtə]	Müll; Abfall
track [træk]	Weg; Pfad
to **disturb** [dɪ'stɜ:b]	stören
site [saɪt]	Ort; Gelände; Schauplatz
to **damage** ['dæmɪdʒ]	schaden; beschädigen
lizard ['lɪzəd]	Echse; Eidechse
deadly ['dedli]	tödlich

1 Safety advice

Complete the sentences. Use the words below.

disturb | netted off | rip currents | on your own | marine stinger | swept out | snake | bushwalking

1. Don't go off into the outback ______________________.
2. Make sure you go with someone who has ______________________ experience.
3. Go to beaches that have been ______________________, so you don't get stung by a ______________________.
4. When you see a ______________________, don't ______________________ it – you might get bitten!
5. Be careful of ______________________! Hundreds of people are ______________________ to sea and are never seen again.

2 Odd word out

Cross out the word that doesn't fit.

1. seashell | ocean | cluster | wave
2. garbage | litter | rubbish | track
3. giant | large | deadly | huge
4. rip current | snake | box jellyfish | lizard
5. site | interior | association | terrace

Station 2: When did your folks get here?

folks *(infml) (pl)* [fəʊks]	Leute
No worries. [ˌnəʊ ˈwʌriz]	Kein Problem.; Gern geschehen.
How are you doing? [ˌhaʊ‿ɑː jə ˈduːɪŋ]	Wie geht es dir/euch/Ihnen?
Nice to meet you. [ˌnaɪs tə ˈmiːt juː]	Nett, dich/euch/Sie kennenzulernen.
Kiwi *(infml)* [ˈkiːwiː]	Neuseeländer/-in
to **trace back** [ˌtreɪs ˈbæk]	zurückverfolgen
ancestor [ˈænsestə]	Vorfahr/-in; Ahn/-in
convict [ˈkɒnvɪkt]	Sträfling
to **bump into sb** [ˌbʌmp‿ˈɪntə]	jmdn. zufällig treffen; *hier:* jmdn. anrempeln
sentence [ˈsentəns]	Verurteilung; Strafmaß
victim [ˈvɪktɪm]	Opfer
used to *(+ infinitive)* [ˈjuːst tə]	pflegte(n) zu; tat(en) früher
to **oppress** [əˈpres]	unterdrücken
indigenous *(fml)* [ɪnˈdɪdʒɪnəs]	einheimisch; heimisch
to **have sth done** [hæv]	etw. machen lassen
to **renovate** [ˈrenəveɪt]	renovieren
leftovers *(pl)* [ˈleftəʊvəz]	Überbleibsel; Überreste
to **allow** [əˈlaʊ]	erlauben; gestatten
to **make** [meɪk]	*hier:* lassen
farewell [ˌfeəˈwel]	Abschied; Abschieds-
to **deliver** [dɪˈlɪvə]	liefern
overseas [ˌəʊvəˈsiːz]	in Übersee; im Ausland
to **host** [həʊst]	ausrichten *(Veranstaltung)*
variety (of) [vəˈraɪəti‿əv]	Vielzahl (an); Vielfalt (von)
celebration [ˌseləˈbreɪʃn]	Feier
to **apply (for)** [əˈplaɪ fə]	sich bewerben (um); beantragen
occupation [ˌɒkjəˈpeɪʃn]	Beruf; Beschäftigung

policy ['pɒləsi]	Politik; politische Linie
restrictive [rɪ'strɪktɪv]	beschränkend; einengend

3 Australia: A multicultural country

Complete the missing words.

Australia is one of the most multicultural countries in the world. Cliff's a☐☐☐☐☐☐☐☐ were the first people who came to Australia; these people are often called 'I☐☐☐☐☐☐☐☐☐ Australians'. At the end of the 18th century, the British founded a penal colony in Australia where they sent their c☐☐☐☐☐☐☐. So, for example, Mike's ancestor, Bill, got a s☐☐☐☐☐☐☐ of 30 years in Australia. In the 1970s, Cam's parents came from Vietnam because people were being o☐☐☐☐☐☐☐☐ there. Today, 25% of the population was born o☐☐☐☐☐☐☐, most of them in the UK, New Zealand and China.

4 What word?

Read the words in the phonetic alphabet and write them down. Use the grid on page 3 for help.

1. [ˌɒkjəˈpeɪʃn]

____

2. [dɪˈlɪvə]

____

3. [ɪnˈdɪdʒɪnəs]

____

4. [ˌfeəˈwel]

____

5 Definitions

Put in the missing words.

1. If you _______________ an old building, a piece of furniture, etc., you repair and paint it.
2. A _______________ is a person who has been attacked, injured or killed.
3. _______________ are items of food that haven't been eaten at the end of a meal.
4. A _______________ is a plan of action which is chosen by a political party, a business, etc.
5. A _______________ is a special event that people organise in order to celebrate something.
6. When you work _______________, you work in a foreign country.

Station 3: The land owns us

value ['vælju:]	Wert
Dreaming ['dri:mɪŋ]	Traumzeit
knowledge *(no pl)* ['nɒlɪdʒ]	Wissen; Kenntnisse
underground ['ʌndəgraʊnd]	unterirdisch
soil [sɔɪl]	Erde; Boden
track [træk]	Spur; Fährte
common ['kɒmən]	gemeinsam
foster ['fɒstə]	Pflege-
to **place** [pleɪs]	unterbringen
senior ['si:niə]	älter
permission [pə'mɪʃn]	Erlaubnis; Genehmigung
disrespectful [ˌdɪsrɪ'spektfl]	respektlos
elder ['eldə]	Älteste/-r
guardian ['gɑ:diən]	Hüter/-in; Wächter/-in
territory ['terɪtri]	Gebiet; Revier; Territorium
childhood ['tʃaɪldhʊd]	Kindheit
anniversary [ˌænɪ'vɜ:sri]	Jubiläum; Jahrestag
to **protest** [prə'test]	protestieren
nomad ['nəʊmæd]	Nomade/Nomadin
no longer [ˌnəʊ 'lɒŋgə]	nicht länger; nicht mehr

Skills: How to structure a radio news report

attack [ə'tæk]	Angriff; Überfall
full [fʊl]	ganz
to **be involved (in)** [bi‿ɪn'vɒlvd‿ɪn]	beteiligt sein (an); involviert sein (in); engagiert sein (in)
newsreader ['nju:sˌri:də]	Nachrichtensprecher/-in
at the scene [ˌət ðə 'si:n]	vor Ort
lifeguard ['laɪfgɑ:d]	Rettungsschwimmer/-in
to **prevent** [prɪ'vent]	verhindern; abhalten
over to ... ['əʊvə tə]	weiter zu …

6 Word search: Aboriginal Australia

Find seven words (↑, ↗, ↓, → or ←) that can be used to describe Aboriginal Australia. Then complete the sentences below with four of them.

S	D	A	M	O	N	S	D	U	E
Y	A	L	X	S	K	Z	P	G	T
R	T	I	K	C	A	R	D	U	Q
O	N	R	A	X	U	E	M	A	K
T	X	R	N	U	L	D	A	R	S
I	T	A	N	W	X	L	L	D	E
R	Z	P	O	T	Q	E	K	I	M
R	U	N	M	L	S	A	Q	A	I
E	K	T	A	E	P	Z	U	N	S
T	D	R	E	A	M	I	N	G	U

1. Before the arrival of the British, the Aboriginal people used to live as ____________________.

2. They used to hunt animals by following their ____________________.

3. The ____________________ stories pass on important ____________________ to later generations.

Story: Nona and me

guilty conscience [ˌgɪlti ˈkɒnʃns]	Schuldbewusstsein; schlechtes Gewissen
to **stand up for sb/sth** [ˌstænd‿ˈʌp fə]	jmdn./etw. verteidigen; für jmdn./etw. einstehen
glimpse [glɪms]	(kurzer/flüchtiger) Blick
determined [dɪˈtɜːmɪnd]	(fest) entschlossen; entschieden; zielstrebig
upright [ˈʌpraɪt]	aufrecht
walk [wɔːk]	Gang
strength [streŋθ]	Stärke; Kraft
rib [rɪb]	Rippe
desperate [ˈdesprət]	verzweifelt; hoffnungslos; ausweglos
to **sigh** [saɪ]	seufzen
to **get ready** [ˌget ˈredi]	sich vorbereiten; sich fertig machen
to **grin** [grɪn]	grinsen
reluctant [rɪˈlʌktnt]	widerstrebend; widerwillig
to **face** [feɪs]	anblicken; sich zuwenden
federation [ˌfedrˈeɪʃn]	Bundesstaat; Föderation
to **raise one's eyes** [ˌreɪz wʌnz‿ˈaɪz]	den Blick heben; aufblicken; hochblicken
scar [skɑː]	Narbe
desk [desk]	Schreibtisch
nod [nɒd]	Nicken
to **nod** [nɒd]	nicken
enthusiastic [ɪnˌθjuːziˈæstɪk]	enthusiastisch; begeistert
university [ˌjuːnɪˈvɜːsəti]	Universität
beat [biːt]	Takt; Rhythmus
to **be related to** [bi rɪˈleɪtɪd tə]	verwandt sein mit
laughter [ˈlɑːftə]	Gelächter; Lachen

soft [sɒft]	weich; sanft
harmless [ˈhɑːmləs]	harmlos; ungefährlich
to **lean forward** [ˌliːn ˈfɔːwəd]	sich nach vorn lehnen
previous [ˈpriːviəs]	früher; vorherig; vorhergehend
fingernail [ˈfɪŋgəneɪl]	Fingernagel
pale [peɪl]	blass
to **shake** [ʃeɪk], **shook** [ʃʊk], **shaken** [ˈʃeɪkn]	schütteln
to **frown** [fraʊn]	die Stirn runzeln
abrupt [əˈbrʌpt]	abrupt
ceiling [ˈsiːlɪŋ]	Zimmerdecke; Decke
fan [fæn]	Ventilator
armchair [ˈɑːmtʃeə]	Sessel
to **glance at** [ˈglɑːns‿ət]	einen Blick werfen auf; blicken auf
grateful [ˈgreɪtfl]	dankbar
awkward [ˈɔːkwəd]	peinlich; ungünstig; ungeschickt; unbeholfen

7 What you can do with your face or head

Find the right infinitives for the descriptions.

1. You move your head up and down: ______________________________
2. You smile widely: ______________________________
3. You have your face pointing towards somebody or something: ______________________________
4. You make a serious, angry or worried expression by bringing your eyebrows closer together: ______________________________

8 Nona and me

Fill in the correct words and find the solution.

1. A … is a view of somebody or something for a very short time.
2. A … is a piece of furniture like a table that you sit at to read, write, work, etc.
3. Being … means that you feel you want to thank someone because he / she has done something for you.
4. A person is … if he or she has skin that is almost white.
5. If they have done something wrong, many people have a guilty …

Solution: You are ______________________________ if you have no hope and are ready to do anything to change the situation you are in.

9 Opposites

Find the opposite of each word. The words are all new in Unit 1.

1. floor ↔ ______________________
2. hard ↔ ______________________
3. next ↔ ______________________
4. welcome ↔ ______________________
5. danger ↔ ______________________
6. in a group ↔ ______________________

10 Positive or negative?

Write the adjectives in the correct part of the grid. They are all new in Unit 1.

upright desperate determined comforting awkward
enthusiastic soft disrespectful

Positive	Negative

11 Phrasal verbs

a) *Find the correct prepostions for the verbs. The phrasal verbs are all new in Unit 1.*

call show trace stand up be involved glance

for in around off at back

1. ______________________________

2. ______________________________

3. ______________________________

4. ______________________________

5. ______________________________

6. ______________________________

b) *Complete the sentences below with phrasal verbs from a). Make sure you use the correct tense.*

1. If you want to go to the city centre, our guide can ______________ you ______________.
2. I can ______________ my ancestors ______________ to the 19th century.
3. After three days, the search for the missing tourist in the outback was ______________.
4. I only heard part of the report, so I can't tell you who ______________ the accident.

12 Synonyms

Write down a word with the same or a similar meaning. All the words are new in Unit 1.

1. alone ➚ ______________________
2. not any more ➚ ______________________
3. garbage ➚ ______________________
4. ground ➚ ______________________
5. party ➚ ______________________
6. abroad ➚ ______________________

13 Check on your ... Australia words

Make a list of the words that describe Australia in Unit 1.

____

____

____

____

____

____

____

____

Text smart 1 A short film

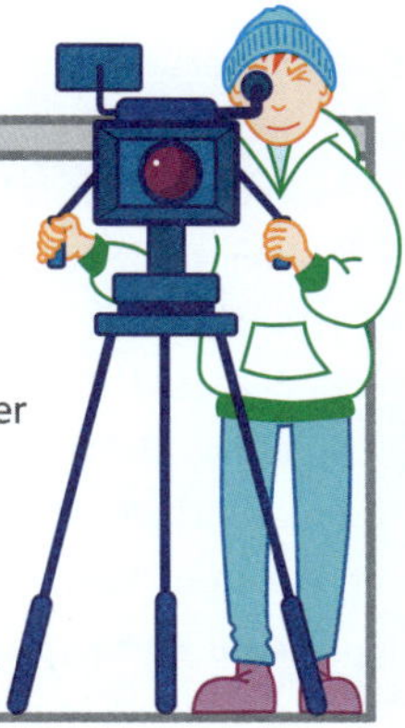

Tip

Filme zu schauen macht Spaß und bietet dir gleichzeitig eine gute Möglichkeit, dein Englisch zu verbessern! Je öfter du Filme auf Englisch anschaust, umso besser wirst du die Schauspieler verstehen. Versuche, dir wichtige Redewendungen für Dialoge zu merken. Du kannst sie später für mündliche Aufgaben oder deine eigene Textproduktion verwenden.

Introduction

key feature [ˌkiː ˈfiːtʃə]	Hauptmerkmal
clip [klɪp]	Clip; Ausschnitt
visual [ˈvɪʒuəl]	visuell; optisch
crew [kruː]	Crew; Besatzung; Mannschaft; Team
appearance [əˈpɪərns]	Erscheinung; Aussehen; Auftritt
cast [kɑːst]	Besetzung; Ensemble
supporting role [səˈpɔːtɪŋ ˌrəʊl]	Nebenrolle
wide shot [ˈwaɪd ˌʃɒt]	Totale *(Kameraeinstellung)*

Station 1: A first look

emotion [ɪˈməʊʃn]	Gefühl; Emotion
misery *(no pl)* [ˈmɪzri]	Elend; Jammer; Not
uncomfortable [ʌnˈkʌmftəbl]	unwohl; unbehaglich; unbequem
tear [tɪə]	Träne
master [ˈmɑːstə]	Herr/-in; Meister/-in
fate [feɪt]	Schicksal; Fügung; Vorsehung

Station 2: Key elements of films

movement ['mu:vmənt]	Bewegung
flirty ['flɜ:ti]	zum Flirten aufgelegt; kokett
extremely [ɪk'stri:mli]	sehr; äußerst
annoyed [ə'nɔɪd]	verärgert
bitchy ['bɪtʃi]	gehässig; gemein
disgusted [dɪs'gʌstɪd]	angeekelt; angewidert
turned off [ˌtɜ:nd‿'ɒf]	abgetörnt
entire [ɪn'taɪə]	gesamt; ganz; komplett
context ['kɒntekst]	Kontext; Zusammenhang
surroundings *(pl)* [sə'raʊndɪŋz]	Umgebung
to **establish** [ɪ'stæblɪʃ]	einführen

Station 3: How to structure film scripts

onlooker ['ɒnˌlʊkə]	Zuschauer/-in
front [frʌnt]	Spitze; vorderer Bereich
back [bæk]	Ende; hinterer Bereich
to **knock** [nɒk]	stoßen; schlagen
to **introduce** [ˌɪntrə'dju:s]	vorstellen
understanding [ˌʌndə'stændɪŋ]	verständnisvoll
hysterical [hɪ'sterɪkl]	hysterisch
rather ['rɑ:ðə]	ziemlich

1 Word families

Find a word from the same word family.

1. emotional → ______________________ (noun)
2. understand → ______________________ (adjective)
3. introduction → ______________________ (verb)

2 Alicia's Hollywood story

Put in the missing words. The synonyms or definitions in brackets will help you.

When Alicia went to Hollywood, she felt that she was no longer the master of her own ______________________ (= what happens to someone). She was ______________________ (= angry) by all the open auditions she had to go to and her life seemed full of ______________________ (= great suffering). But then she was offered a ______________________ (= not the most important role in a film) in a smaller production. What luck! Her role was a real challenge since she had to play a woman who was very ______________________ (= being over-excited and extremely emotional), but she did so well that next she got a role in one of the bigger movies!

3 Check on your ... film words

Make a list of the film words you learned in Text smart 1.

____

____

____

____

Unit 2 The good life?

Tip

Beim Vokabellernen kann es dir helfen, Wortfelder zu einem Thema anzulegen, um die Wörter im Zusammenhang zu lernen. In Unit 2 bieten sich hier z. B. die Wortfelder „Jobsuche / Bewerbung“ oder „Soziales Engagement“ an.

Introduction

fulfilling [fʊlˈfɪlɪŋ]	erfüllend; befriedigend
materialistic [məˌtɪəriəˈlɪstɪk]	materialistisch
meaningful [ˈmiːnɪŋfl]	bedeutsam; wichtig
adventurous [ədˈventʃrəs]	abenteuerlich; unternehmungslustig; wagemutig; experimentierfreudig
satisfaction [ˌsætɪsˈfækʃn]	Zufriedenheit
boredom [ˈbɔːdəm]	Langeweile
curiosity [ˌkjʊəriˈɒsəti]	Neugier
desirable [dɪˈzaɪərəbl]	wünschenswert; erstrebenswert

Station 1: Best summer ever!

to **encourage** [ɪnˈkʌrɪdʒ]	unterstützen; ermutigen
to **raise** [reɪz]	(er)wecken *(Interesse)*; aufwerfen *(Fragen)*
opportunity [ˌɒpəˈtjuːnəti]	Chance; Gelegenheit; Möglichkeit
assistant counsellor [əˌsɪstnt ˈkaʊnslə]	Hilfsbetreuer/-in
senior counsellor [ˌsiːniə ˈkaʊnslə]	leitender Betreuer/leitende Betreuerin; ranghohe/-r Minister/-in

to **be passionate about sth** [bi 'pæʃnət əˌbaʊt]	etw. leidenschaftlich gern tun; eine Leidenschaft für etw. haben; für etw. brennen
testimonial [ˌtestɪ'məʊniəl]	Erfahrungsbericht
qualification [ˌkwɒlɪfɪ'keɪʃn]	Qualifikation; Befähigung; Abschluss; Schulabschluss
to **require** [rɪ'kwaɪə]	benötigen; erfordern
applicant ['æplɪkənt]	Bewerber/-in
position [pə'zɪʃn]	Stelle; Position
to **be supposed to** *(+ inf)* [bi sə'pəʊzd tə]	sollen
to **set a good example** [set‿ə ˌgʊd‿ɪg'zɑ:mpl]	ein Vorbild sein
at all times [ˌət‿ɔ:l 'taɪmz]	immer; jederzeit; stets
to **be expected to** *(+ inf)* [bi ɪk'spektɪd tə]	sollen
to **be a team player** [ˌbi‿ə 'ti:m ˌpleɪə]	gern im Team arbeiten
responsibility [rɪˌspɒnsə'bɪləti]	Verantwortung; Aufgabe
CV *(Curriculum Vitae)* [ˌsi:'vi: (kəˌrɪkjələm 'vi:taɪ)]	Lebenslauf
application letter [ˌæplɪ'keɪʃn ˌletə]	Bewerbungsschreiben
gender ['dʒendə]	Geschlecht
employer [ɪm'plɔɪə]	Arbeitgeber/-in
focused ['fəʊkəst]	zielgerichtet
all-rounder [ɔ:l'raʊndə]	Alleskönner/-in; Multitalent
to **stand out (from)** [ˌstænd‿'aʊt]	sich abheben (von); herausragen (aus)
weakness ['wi:knəs]	Schwäche
stereotype ['steriəʊtaɪp]	Klischee; Stereotyp
gender stereotyping ['dʒendə ˌsteriəʊtaɪpɪŋ]	geschlechtsspezifische Klischees

to **consider** [kən'sɪdə]	betrachten; erwägen
engineering [ˌendʒɪ'nɪərɪŋ]	Technik; Maschinenbau
GCSE *(= General Certificate of Secondary Education)* [ˌdʒi:si:es'i: (ˌdʒenrl səˌtɪfɪkət‿əv ˌsekəndri‿edʒʊ'keɪʃn)]	*allg. Abschluss der weiterführenden Schulen in GB*
to **list** [lɪst]	auflisten; nennen
healthcare ['helθkeə]	Gesundheitsversorgung
female ['fi:meɪl]	weiblich
construction worker [kən'strʌkʃn ˌwɜ:kə]	Bauarbeiter/-in
profession [prə'feʃn]	Beruf
male [meɪl]	männlich
to **associate** [ə'səʊʃieɪt]	assoziieren; verbinden
(business) executive ['bɪznɪs ɪgˌzekjətɪv]	Geschäftsführer/-in; Manager/-in; gehobene Führungskraft
firefighter ['faɪəˌfaɪtə]	Feuerwehrmann/-frau
sales assistant ['seɪlz‿əˌsɪstnt]	Verkäufer/-in
nationality [ˌnæʃn'æləti]	Nationalität; Staatsangehörigkeit
comprehensive school [kɒmprɪ'hensɪv ˌsku:l]	Gesamtschule
organiser ['ɔ:gənaɪzə]	Organisator/-in
hard-working [ˌhɑ:d'wɜ:kɪŋ]	fleißig
people skills *(pl)* ['pi:pl ˌskɪlz]	soziale Kompetenz
reference ['refrns]	Referenz; Referenzschreiben
request [rɪ'kwest]	Anfrage; Nachfrage
common ['kɒmən]	üblich; verbreitet; gängig
with reference to [wɪð 'refrns tə]	bezugnehmend auf
hopefully ['həʊpfli]	hoffentlich
therefore ['ðeəfɔ:]	deshalb; deswegen; daher; somit
moreover [mɔ:r'əʊvə]	überdies; außerdem
addition [ə'dɪʃn]	Zusatz; Ergänzung

(job) interview ['dʒɒb ˌɪntəvjuː]	Vorstellungsgespräch
Yours sincerely [ˌjɔːz sɪn'sɪəli]	Mit freundlichen Grüßen
signature ['sɪgnətʃə]	Unterschrift
enclosure [ɪn'kləʊʒə]	Anlage; Beilage
attachment [ə'tætʃmənt]	Anhang
furthermore [ˌfɜːðə'mɔː]	überdies; außerdem
nevertheless [ˌnevəðə'les]	trotzdem; dennoch; nichtsdestoweniger
unfortunately [ʌn'fɔːtʃnətli]	leider; unglücklicherweise

1 Word search: Job applications

Find seven job application words (↑, ↗, ↓ or ←) and complete the sentences on page 30 with five of them. Make sure you use the right form of the nouns.

I	R	E	Y	O	L	P	M	E	X
S	N	X	T	K	A	M	C	S	T
Z	A	T	M	Q	R	N	L	S	N
G	L	N	E	I	E	X	T	E	A
E	K	W	T	R	U	S	L	N	C
N	I	K	E	M	V	B	A	K	I
D	E	F	S	S	T	I	U	A	L
E	E	N	U	A	B	X	E	E	P
R	M	I	L	T	T	Q	R	W	P
T	N	E	M	H	C	A	T	T	A

1. Unfortunately, I didn't get the job. There were too many ______________________ and I wasn't even invited for an ______________________.
2. We've been talking a lot about your strengths. Let's talk about your ______________________ too.
3. I don't think that only men can be electricians. That's an example of ______________________ stereotyping.
4. ______________________ are available on request.

2 Word pairs: It's all about jobs

Draw lines to make word pairs.

1. construction	a) skills
2. sales	b) stereotyping
3. job	c) worker
4. people	d) executive
5. gender	e) assistant
6. business	f) interview

3 Say it in a different way

Write down the missing word or phrase to make a sentence with the same or a similar meaning.

1. Moreover, I would like to mention my experience with children.

   → ______________________________, I would like to mention my experience with children.

2. If you've applied for a job, make sure that you can always be contacted.

   → If you've applied for a job, make sure that you can be contacted ______________________________.

3. Some young people find it hard to choose a suitable occupation.

   → Some young people find it hard to choose a suitable ______________________________.

4. Having a part-time job gives you a good chance to find out what is needed in a 'real' job.

   → Having a part-time job offers you a good ______________________________ to find out what is ______________________________ in a 'real' job.

4 Odd sound out

Cross out the word with the sound that doesn't fit.

1. **[iː]** weakness | female | require | meaningful
2. **[æ]** satisfaction | gender | passionate | applicant
3. **[ɔː]** boredom | moreover | organiser | consider
4. **[eɪ]** application | male | firefighter | raise

5 Word families

Complete the sentences with a word from the same word family as the word in brackets.

1. Try to be more ______________________________ (focus).

   It's your own ______________________________

   (responsible) to prepare for the job interview in time.

2. Men can be nurses and flight attendants too. It's unfair

   that many people ______________________________

   (association) these jobs with women.

3. I felt good after the interview. ______________________________

   (hope), I will get the job.

4. When you've finished your application letter, don't forget your

   ______________________________ (to sign).

5. Being a firefighter wouldn't be the right job for me. I'm not a

   very ______________________________ (adventure) person.

Station 2: The cocoa controversy

cocoa ['kəʊkəʊ]	Kakao
controversy ['kɒntrəvɜ:si]	Kontroverse; Auseinandersetzung
quantity ['kwɒntɪti]	Menge; Quantität
cosmetics *(pl)* [kɒz'metɪks]	Kosmetik
to **provide** [prə'vaɪd]	liefern; bereit stellen
poverty line ['pɒvəti ˌlaɪn]	Armutsgrenze
poverty ['pɒvəti]	Armut
physical ['fɪzɪkl]	physisch; körperlich
to **harvest** ['hɑ:vɪst]	ernten
bean [bi:n]	Bohne
to **force** [fɔ:s]	zwingen
plantation [plæn'teɪʃn]	Plantage
to **justify** ['dʒʌstɪfaɪ]	rechtfertigen
exhausted [ɪg'zɔ:stɪd]	erschöpft
to **chop** [tʃɒp]	hacken; klein schneiden
pod [pɒd]	Hülse; Schote
machete [mə'ʃeti]	Machete; Buschmesser
to **dump** [dʌmp]	abladen
onto ['ɒntə]	auf … hinauf
trade [treɪd]	Handel
march [mɑ:tʃ]	Marsch; Kundgebung
to **catch oneself doing sth** [kætʃ]	sich (selbst) dabei ertappen, wie …
commitment [kə'mɪtmənt]	Bindung; Verpflichtung; Engagement
volunteer [ˌvɒlən'tɪə]	Freiwillige/-r; Ehrenamtliche/-r
selfish ['selfɪʃ]	selbstsüchtig; egoistisch
involvement [ɪn'vɒlvmənt]	Engagement; Beteiligung
to **volunteer** [ˌvɒlən'tɪə]	eine ehrenamtliche Tätigkeit übernehmen

religious [rɪˈlɪdʒəs]	religiös; gläubig
the elderly [ði ˈeldəli]	ältere Menschen; Senioren
the homeless [ðə ˈhəʊmləs]	Obdachlose
the disabled [ðə dɪˈseɪbld]	Behinderte
volunteer [ˌvɒlənˈtɪə]	freiwillig; ehrenamtlich
gap year [ˈgæp ˌjɪə]	*ein Jahr Auszeit (zwischen Schule und Ausbildung/Studium), das oft für einen freiwilligen ökologischen oder sozialen Dienst genutzt wird*

6 Nouns into verbs

Find the verbs that belong to the same word family as the nouns.

1. involvement ➚ ______________________
2. volunteer ➚ ______________________
3. harvest ➚ ______________________
4. plantation ➚ ______________________

7 What word?

Read the words in the phonetic alphabet and write them down. Use the grid on page 3 for help.

1. [ɪgˈzɔːstɪd] ______________________
2. [ˌvɒlənˈtɪə] ______________________
3. [ˈkɒntrəvɜːsi] ______________________
4. [rɪˈlɪdʒəs] ______________________

8 The cocoa controversy

Complete the text. Use the words below and make sure you use the right form of the verbs.

physically | dump | poverty line | pods
chop | plantations | cocoa | provide
machetes | cosmetics | force | beans

Although Ivory Coast ____________________ about 35% of the world's ____________________, which is a main ingredient for chocolate and for many ____________________, 40% of the population lives below the ____________________. This situation ____________________ a lot of children to work on the cocoa ____________________ to help their families. Their job is to climb the trees and ____________________ down the cocoa ____________________ with their huge ____________________, which is very dangerous and ____________________ difficult for them. Other children have to carry heavy containers full of cocoa ____________________ and ____________________ the contents onto a large truck.

Station 3: I do remember how it feels ...

wisdom *(no pl)* ['wɪzdəm]	Weisheit; Klugheit
carpenter ['kɑ:pntə]	Schreiner/-in; Zimmermann
not only ... but (also) [nɒt‿ˌəʊnli ... bʌt‿'ɔ:lsəʊ]	nicht nur ... sondern (auch)
to **stack** [stæk]	stapeln
to **go by** [ˌgəʊ‿'baɪ]	vorbeigehen
left over [left‿'əʊvə]	übrig
pay [peɪ]	Lohn; Gehalt
tax [tæks]	Steuer; Abgabe
wage [weɪdʒ]	Lohn
patient ['peɪʃnt]	geduldig
rarely ['reəli]	selten
top [tɒp]	Spitzen-; oberster; bester
law [lɔ:]	Gesetz; Recht
know-it-all ['nəʊɪtɔ:l]	Besserwisser/-in
brief [bri:f]	kurz
to **limit to** ['lɪmɪt tə]	limitieren auf; begrenzen auf; beschränken auf
investment [ɪn'vesmənt]	Einlage; Beteiligung; Investition
buddy *(infml)* ['bʌdi]	Kumpel
to **be made up of/from** [bi meɪd‿'ʌp‿əv/frəm]	zusammengesetzt sein aus; bestehen aus
toothbrush ['tu:θbrʌʃ]	Zahnbürste
no sooner [nəʊ 'su:nə]	kaum
colleague ['kɒli:g]	Kollege/Kollegin
to **suit sb** [su:t]	(zu) jmdm. passen; jmdm. stehen

Skills: Making a good impression

candidate ['kændɪdət]	Bewerber/-in; Kandidat/-in
to **emphasise** ['emfəsaɪz]	betonen
tricky ['trɪki]	schwierig; kompliziert

Unit task: Job interviews for a summer camp

helper ['helpə] Helfer/-in

9 Definitions

Put in the missing words.

1. If something is difficult, you can also say it's

   ______________________________.

2. You use a ______________________________ to clean your teeth.

3. A person that you work with is called a

   ______________________________.

4. ____________________ are rules, usually made by a government,

   that are used to order the way in which a society behaves.

10 Odd word out

Cross out the word that doesn't fit.

1. firefighter | employer | pilot | carpenter
2. work | job | applicant | position
3. machete | bean | cocoa | pod
4. commitment | tax | pay | investment
5. difficult | tricky | complicated | common

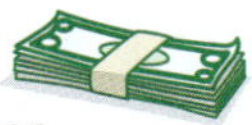

Story: The Giver

giver ['gɪvə]	Geber/-in; Spender/-in
to **regulate** ['regjəleɪt]	regeln; regulieren
assignment [ə'saɪnmənt]	Aufgabe; Auftrag; Mission
destiny ['destɪni]	Schicksal; Fügung; Vorsehung
to **assign** [ə'saɪn]	zuordnen; übertragen
to **acknowledge** [ək'nɒlɪdʒ]	anerkennen; einräumen
to **fit in** [ˌfɪt‿'ɪn]	hineinpassen; sich einfügen
to **standardize** *(AE)* ['stændədaɪz]	standardisieren; vereinheitlichen
to **honor** *(AE)* ['ɒnə]	ehren; würdigen; auszeichnen
to **determine** [dɪ'tɜ:mɪn]	bestimmen; ermitteln
throughout [θru'aʊt]	während; überall in
satisfied ['sætɪsfaɪd]	zufrieden; befriedigt
apology [ə'pɒlədʒi]	Entschuldigung
to **select** [sɪ'lekt]	auswählen; aussuchen
receiver [rɪ'si:və]	Empfänger/-in; *hier:* Hüter/-in
sheet [ʃi:t]	Blatt
session ['seʃn]	Sitzung; Stunde
ability [ə'bɪləti]	Fähigkeit
to **transmit** [trænz'mɪt]	übertragen
sir [sɜ:]	mein Herr *(Anrede)*
impatient [ɪm'peɪʃnt]	ungeduldig
laugh [lɑ:f]	Lachen
distant ['dɪstnt]	entfernt; distanziert
sameness ['seɪmnəs]	Gleichheit; Gleichförmigkeit
to **slow down** [ˌsləʊ 'daʊn]	langsamer werden; bremsen
ordinary ['ɔ:dnri]	gewöhnlich; normal
curious ['kjʊəriəs]	neugierig
to **make a choice** [ˌmeɪk‿ə 'tʃɔɪs]	eine Wahl treffen

to **matter** ['mætə]	von Bedeutung sein; etw. ausmachen
to **dare** [deə]	wagen
mate [meɪt]	Partner/-in
literature ['lɪtrətʃə]	Literatur

11 Guess the right verb

Complete the sentences. Make sure you use the right form of the verbs.

standardize | select | make a choice | matter | dare | acknowledge

1. The pay I get for my job doesn't ______________________ to me that much; I want to be happy with what I'm doing.
2. You need to ______________________ the fact that somebody else has been ______________________ to join the team. Maybe it will be your turn next time.
3. Today school tests are often ______________________, so that the results can be compared to those of other schools.
4. You can't do both jobs at the same time, you need to ______________________.
5. You should call them and ask if you got the job. – No, I don't ______________________ to do that. They might get angry.

12 Verbs into nouns

Find the nouns that belong to the same word family as the verbs.

1. to be able to → ______________________
2. to assign → ______________________
3. to laugh → ______________________
4. to apologize → ______________________

13 Positive or negative?

Write the adjectives in the correct part of the grid. They are all new in Unit 2.

satisfied | hard-working | fulfilling | exhausted

patient | selfish | focused | meaningful | impatient

Positive	Negative

14 Opposites

Find the opposite of each word. The words are all new in Unit 2.

1. lazy ↔ ______________________
2. impatient ↔ ______________________
3. often ↔ ______________________
4. male ↔ ______________________
5. the young ↔ ______________________
6. strength ↔ ______________________

15 Check on your ... job words

Make a list of the words you learned in Unit 2 to talk about jobs and applications.

____

____

____

____

____

____

____

____

Text smart 2 Informative texts

Tip

Wenn es wie in den *Text smarts* um die Produktion bestimmter Textsorten geht, hilft es dir, eine Liste mit *Useful phrases* anzulegen, die du später für deine eigenen Texte verwenden kannst.

Introduction

earthquake ['ɜ:θkweɪk]	Erdbeben
review [rɪ'vju:]	Kritik
criticism ['krɪtɪsɪzm]	Kritik

Station 1: How to: Write a text summary

entitled [ɪn'taɪtld]	mit dem Titel
around [ə'raʊnd]	ungefähr; etwa
enslavement [ɪn'sleɪvmənt]	Versklavung
to **be unable to do sth** [bi‿ʌn'eɪbl tə]	unfähig sein, etw. zu tun; nicht in der Lage sein, etw. zu tun
to **conclude** [kən'klu:d]	enden; schließen; schlussfolgern
journalist ['dʒɜ:nlɪst]	Journalist/-in
injured ['ɪndʒəd]	verletzt
irrelevant [ɪ'reləvnt]	irrelevant; nicht von Bedeutung
study ['stʌdi]	Studie; Untersuchung
in particular [ˌɪn pə'tɪkjələ]	im besonderen
biological [ˌbaɪə'lɒdʒɪkl]	biologisch
deprivation [ˌdeprɪ'veɪʃn]	Entbehrung; Entzug
currently ['kʌrntli]	momentan

to **recruit** [rɪ'kru:t]	rekrutieren; anwerben; einstellen
cycle ['saɪkl]	Zyklus; Kreislauf
rise [raɪz]	Anstieg; Zunahme
fall [fɔ:l]	Abnahme
gene [dʒi:n]	Gen
cognitive ['kɒgnətɪv]	kognitiv
performance [pə'fɔ:məns]	Leistung
metabolism [mə'tæblɪzm]	Stoffwechsel
and so on [ənd 'səʊ‿ɒn]	und so weiter
mismatch ['mɪsmætʃ]	Missverhältnis
well-suited (to doing sth) [ˌwel'su:tɪd]	geeignet (für/um zu); passend (für)
to **rise** [raɪz]	aufstehen
deprived [dɪ'praɪvd]	beraubt; entzogen
well-known [ˌwel'nəʊn]	(wohl) bekannt
researcher [rɪ'sɜ:tʃə]	Forscher/-in
evidence *(no pl)* ['evɪdns]	Beweis; Beleg; Beweismaterial
to **point to** ['pɔɪnt tə]	deuten auf; hindeuten auf; zeigen auf
outcome ['aʊtkʌm]	Ergebnis; Resultat

Station 2: How to: Write a text analysis

to **relate to** [rɪ'leɪt tə]	nachvollziehen; sich identifizieren mit; verstehen
objective [əb'dʒektɪv]	objektiv
scientific [ˌsaɪən'tɪfɪk]	wissenschaftlich; naturwissenschaftlich
to **aim to do sth** [eɪm]	anstreben; abzielen auf
plenty of ['plenti‿əv]	eine Menge
to **quote** [kwəʊt]	zitieren
balance ['bæləns]	Gleichgewicht
relevant ['reləvnt]	relevant; von Bedeutung

1 Definitions

Put in the missing words.

1. If you want to say 'now'/'at this moment', you can also say '________________________________'.
2. An ________________________________ is a sudden shaking of the earth's surface.
3. A ________________________________ is a report in a newspaper or magazine, or on the internet, in which you give your opinion about a book, film, etc.
4. A person whose job is to collect and write news stories is called a ________________________________.
5. The ________________________________ of an activity or process is the final result of that activity or process.
6. If you ________________________________ someone, you try to persuade him / her to work for a company or to join an organisation.

2 Find the missing word

Put in the missing words.

1. study – student research – ____________
2. to study – study to perform – ____________
3. freedom – enslavement rise – ____________
4. rise – to rise conclusion – ____________

3 Check on your ... summary phrases

Make a list of phrases you can use to write a summary.

____

____

____

____

____

____

____

____

____

____

____

Across cultures 2 The language of tolerance and respect

Tip

Bei Themen wie „Toleranz und Respekt", die in der heutigen Zeit eine wichtige Rolle spielen und daher immer wieder angesprochen werden, lohnt es sich, wenn du dir eine Liste mit persönlichem Vokabular anlegst. Das können Wörter oder Phrasen sein, die du wichtig findest, um über das Thema zu sprechen, oder solche, die du dir schwer merken kannst. Deine Liste kannst du im weiteren Verlauf der Arbeit mit Green Line beliebig erweitern.

tolerance ['tɒlrns]	Toleranz
goat [gəʊt]	Ziege
beyond [bi'ɒnd]	jenseits; über … hinaus
to **free** [fri:]	befreien
various ['veəriəs]	verschieden; verschiedenartig
prejudice ['predʒədɪs]	Vorurteil
mainstream ['meɪnstrɪ:m]	Masse; Durchschnitt; Massen-; Durchschnitts-
to **be prejudiced against sb/sth** [bi 'predʒədɪst əˌgenst]	voreingenommen sein gegenüber jmdm./etw.
race [reɪs]	Rasse
to **provoke** [prə'vəʊk]	provozieren; hervorrufen
willingly ['wɪlɪŋli]	gern; freiwillig
unwillingly [ʌn'wɪlɪŋli]	ungern; widerwillig
diversity [daɪ'vɜ:səti]	Vielfalt; Verschiedenheit
street fair ['stri:t feə]	Straßenfest
pedestrian [pɪ'destriən]	Fußgänger/-in; Fußgänger-
kiss [kɪs]	Kuss
respectful [rɪ'spektfl]	respektvoll

privacy ['prɪvəsi]	Privatsphäre
to **assume** [ə'sjuːm]	annehmen
acceptable [ək'septəbl]	akzeptabel; annehmbar
to **bring up** [ˌbrɪŋ‿'ʌp]	zur Sprache bringen
same-sex [ˌseɪm'seks]	gleichgeschlechtlich
lesbian ['lezbiən]	lesbisch; Lesbe
straight [streɪt]	heterosexuell
to **come out** [ˌkʌm‿'aʊt]	sich outen
sensitive ['sensɪtɪv]	sensibel; empfindsam; heikel
problematic [ˌprɒblə'mætɪk]	problematisch; schwierig
vulgar ['vʌlgə]	vulgär; gewöhnlich
to **embarrass** [ɪm'bærəs]	in Verlegenheit bringen
to **spread** [spred], **spread** [spred], **spread** [spred]	(sich) verbreiten
horrible ['hɒrəbl]	schrecklich; furchtbar
rumour ['ruːmə]	Gerücht
to **take sth the wrong way** [ˌteɪk‿ðə rɒŋ 'weɪ]	etw. falsch auffassen; etw. in den falschen Hals bekommen
to **offend** [ə'fend]	beleidigen; verletzen

1 Word families

Find a word from the same word family.

1. to accept ➚ ______________________ (adjective)
2. freedom ➚ ______________________ (verb)
3. horror ➚ ______________________ (adjective)
4. tolerant ➚ ______________________ (noun)
5. problem ➚ ______________________ (adjective)

2 Tolerance and respect

Fill in the correct words and find the solution.

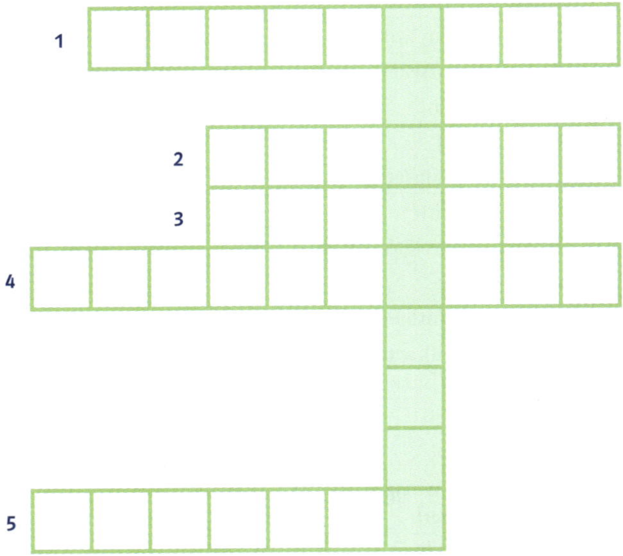

1. Women still face … in the workplace.
2. A tweet might … a lot of reaction, either positive or negative.
3. It can … other people if you make jokes about their friends.
4. If you have an individual lifestyle, you're not into the …
5. If you want others to respect your …, you need to respect theirs.

Solution: We speak of cultural ________________
when people of different cultures, nationalities, languages, sexual orientations and religions live in the same community.

3 Phrasal verbs

a) *Find the correct prepostions for the verbs below and write down the phrasal verbs. Use each preposition only once. The phrasal verbs are all new in Green Line 5.*

be prejudiced | slow | go | stand | be passionate | fit | bring | come

by | out | down | up | against | about | in | out

1. ______________________
2. ______________________
3. ______________________
4. ______________________
5. ______________________
6. ______________________
7. ______________________
8. ______________________

b) *Complete the text below with phrasal verbs from a).*

As a teenager, Ivy never wanted to ______________________ from her friends at school, but tried hard to ______________________. Until one day she realised that she liked girls more than boys. It took her a long time to ______________________ because she knew that some of her classmates were ______________________ gay people. In the end, they reacted much better than she thought and today Ivy is ______________________ fighting for gay rights.

Unit 3 California dreaming

Tip

Bei Wörtern wie *drought* oder *entrepreneur* wirst du vielleicht über die Aussprache stolpern. Sieh dir die Lautschrift genau an und sage dir die Wörter mehrmals laut vor. So kannst du dir die Aussprache besser einprägen.

Introduction

skatepark ['skeɪtpɑ:k]	Skateboardanlage
headquarters *(pl)* [ˌhed'kwɔ:təz]	Zentrale; Hauptsitz
lounge [laʊndʒ]	Lounge; Aufenthaltsraum
skateboarder ['skeɪtbɔ:də]	Skateboardfahrer/-in
tendency ['tendənsi]	Tendenz
Mexican ['meksɪkn]	mexikanisch; Mexikanisch; aus Mexiko; Mexikaner/-in
pot [pɒt]	Topf
reason ['ri:zn]	Vernunft; Verstand
governor ['gʌvnə]	Gouverneur/-in
to **observe** [əb'zɜ:v]	beobachten; beachten; befolgen

Station 1: Hollywood hopes

aspiring [ə'spaɪrɪŋ]	aufstrebend
luck [lʌk]	Glück
to **stroll** [strəʊl]	schlendern; bummeln; spazieren
that way [ˌðæt 'weɪ]	so; auf diese Weise
glitz and glamor *(AE) (no pl)* [ˌglɪts‿n‿'glæmə]	Glanz und Glamour

to **keep one's head above water** [ˌkiːp wʌnz ˌhed‿əbʌv ˈwɔːtə]	sich über Wasser halten
to **showcase one's talent** [ˌʃəʊkeɪs wʌnz ˈtælənt]	sein Talent unter Beweis stellen
lucky day [ˌlʌki ˈdeɪ]	Glückstag
cattle call *(AE)* [ˈkætl ˌkɔːl]	Vorspielen; Vorsingen
wannabe *(infml)* [ˈwɒnəbi]	Möchtegern; Möchtegern-
to **pack up** [ˈpæk‿ʌp]	zusammenpacken
to **chalk sth up to experience** [ˌtʃɔːk‿ʌp tə ɪkˈspɪəriəns]	etw. als Erfahrung verbuchen
premiere [ˈpremieə]	Premiere; Uraufführung
to **cause a stir** [ˌkɔːz‿ə ˈstɜː]	für Aufsehen sorgen
RV park *(AE)* [ˌɑːˈviː ˌpɑːk]	Campingplatz
to **shoot** [ʃuːt]	drehen *(Film)*
to **explode** [ɪkˈspləʊd]	explodieren
trailer *(AE)* [ˈtreɪlə]	Wohnwagen
extra [ˈekstrə]	Statist/-in; Komparse/Komparsin
what it's all about [ˌwɒt‿ɪts‿ɔːl‿əˈbaʊt]	worum es geht
effort [ˈefət]	Bemühung; Mühe
to **pursue** [pəˈsjuː]	verfolgen
persistent [pəˈsɪstnt]	hartnäckig; ausdauernd; beharrlich
relaxed [rɪˈlækst]	entspannt; locker; gelassen
suitable [ˈsuːtəbl]	geeignet; passend
agent [ˈeɪdʒnt]	Agent/-in
to **catch** [kætʃ], **caught** [kɔːt], **caught** [kɔːt]	nehmen *(Zug, Bus)*
backstage [ˌbækˈsteɪdʒ]	backstage; hinter der Bühne
memorable [ˈmemrəbl]	denkwürdig; unvergesslich
to **nominate** [ˈnɒmɪneɪt]	nominieren; ernennen

founder ['faʊndə]	Gründer/-in
to **comprise** [kəm'praɪz]	umfassen; beinhalten; einschließen
producer [prə'dju:sə]	Produzent/-in
contribution [ˌkɒntrɪ'bju:ʃn]	Beitrag; Beteiligung
as long as [əz 'lɒŋ‿əz]	solange
nominee [ˌnɒmɪ'ni:]	vorgeschlagener Kandidat/ vorgeschlagene Kandidatin
to **approve** [ə'pru:v]	anerkennen; gutheißen; genehmigen
nomination [ˌnɒmɪ'neɪʃn]	Nominierung; Ernennung
in honor of *(AE)* [ɪn‿'ɒnər‿əv]	zu Ehren
animated ['ænɪmeɪtɪd]	Zeichentrick-

1 Word friends

Draw lines to match the words and phrases you can use to talk about Hollywood.

1. chalk
2. cause
3. try
4. showcase
5. keep
6. shoot

a) one's luck
b) sth up to experience
c) a scene
d) one's head above water
e) a stir
f) one's talent

2 Hollywood Dream Factory

Complete the text. Use the words below.

cattle calls | effort | agent | premieres | aspiring | showcase their talent | glitz and glamor | luck | pursue | keep their head above water

Many ______________________ young actors move to Hollywood to try their ______________________ there. They dream of movie ______________________ and a life of ______________________, but most of them need to make a great ______________________ to ______________________ their dream. Sometimes they wait for hours at ______________________ before it's their turn to ______________________, and very often they have a day job that helps them to ______________________.

If they're lucky, they find an ______________________ who helps them to get their first big role.

3 A mind map: Describing people in a positive way

Make a mind map with adjectives you can use to describe people. Use adjectives from Station 1 and words you've already learned.

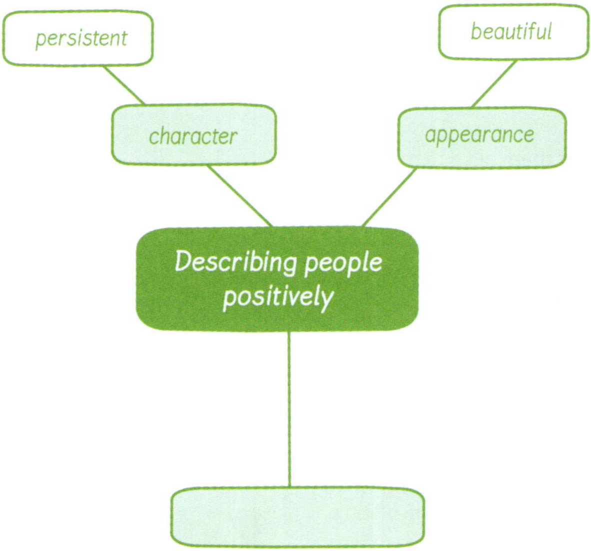

Station 2: A golden state?

golden ['gəʊldn]	golden; Gold-
GDP [ˌdʒiːdiːˈpiː]	BIP *(= Bruttoinlandsprodukt)*
income ['ɪnkʌm]	Einkommen
explorer [ɪk'splɔːrə]	Forscher/-in; Forschungsreisende/-r; Entdecker/-in
to **be said to** *(+ inf)* [bi 'sed tə]	sollen; gelten als
to **exist** [ɪg'zɪst]	existieren; bestehen
wealth [welθ]	Reichtum; Vermögen
Californian [ˌkælɪ'fɔːniən]	kalifornisch; Kalifornier/-in
Gold Rush ['gəʊld ˌrʌʃ]	Goldrausch
precious ['preʃəs]	wertvoll; kostbar
metal ['metl]	Metall
to **boom** [buːm]	florieren; boomen
to **remain** [rɪ'meɪn]	bleiben
sunny ['sʌni]	sonnig
attraction [ə'trækʃn]	Anziehung; Anziehungskraft
northern ['nɔːðən]	nördlich; Nord-
start-up company ['stɑːtʌp ˌkʌmpəni]	Start-up(-Unternehmen); Unternehmensgründung
dot-com bubble [ˌdɒtkɒm 'bʌbl]	Internetblase; Dotcom-Blase
to **burst** [bɜːst], **burst** [bɜːst], **burst** [bɜːst]	bersten; platzen
boom [buːm]	wirtschaftlicher Aufschwung; Boom; Hochkonjunktur
leading ['liːdɪŋ]	führend
worldwide [ˌwɜːld'waɪd]	weltweit
agriculture ['ægrɪkʌltʃə]	Landwirtschaft; Agrikultur
fortune ['fɔːtʃuːn]	Vermögen; Reichtum
to **last** [lɑːst]	dauern; andauern; anhalten

shortage [ˈʃɔːtɪdʒ]	Knappheit; Mangel
drought [draʊt]	Dürre; Trockenheit
to **urge sb to do sth** [ɜːdʒ]	jmdn. zu etw. drängen
cultivation [ˌkʌltɪˈveɪʃn]	Anbau
Hispanic [hɪˈspænɪk]	lateinamerikanisch; Latino/Latina; Hispano-Amerikaner/-in
border [ˈbɔːdə]	Grenze
to **guard** [gɑːd]	bewachen
to **close down** [ˌkləʊz ˈdaʊn]	den Betrieb einstellen; schließen
silicon [ˈsɪlɪkən]	Silizium
component [kəmˈpəʊnənt]	Bestandteil; Komponente
device [dɪˈvaɪs]	Gerät; Vorrichtung
to **be based** [bi ˈbeɪst]	ansässig sein
agricultural [ˌægrɪˈkʌltʃrl]	landwirtschaftlich
entrepreneur [ˌɒntrəprəˈnɜː]	Unternehmer/-in
strawberry [ˈstrɔːbri]	Erdbeere
grape [greɪp]	Traube
to **export** [ɪkˈspɔːt]	exportieren; ausführen
minimum wage [ˌmɪnɪməm ˈweɪdʒ]	Mindestlohn
seasonal [ˈsiːznl]	saisonal; jahreszeitlich bedingt
That doesn't pay my rent. [ˌdət dʌznt ˌpeɪ maɪ ˈrent]	Davon kann ich meine Miete nicht bezahlen.
decade [ˈdekeɪd]	Jahrzehnt
Latino [ləˈtiːnəʊ]	lateinamerikanisch

4 California's economy

Fill in the correct words and find the solution.

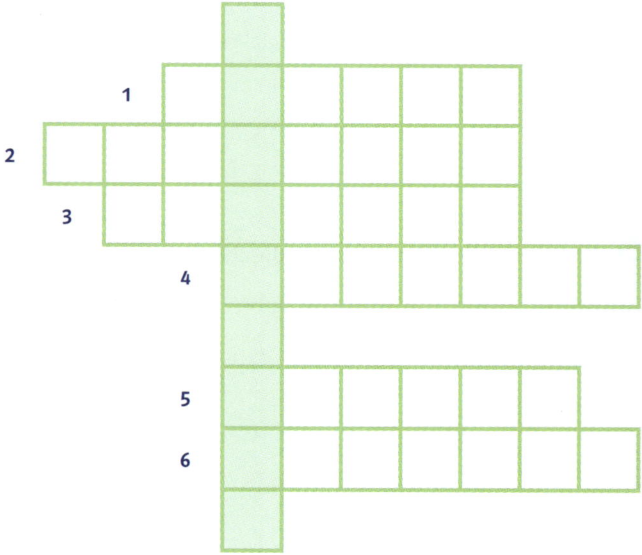

1. California's nickame is the … State.
2. When there isn't enough of something that is needed, we call this a …
3. … is a chemical element that is used in making computers.
4. The … in California caused serious problems for farmers because there wasn't enough water.
5. '…' is the amount of money you earn from work, for example.
6. After the start of many new web businesses in the 1990s, it wasn't long before the … bubble burst.

Solution: This is another word for 'all around the world'.

____

5 Odd sound out

Cross out the word with the sound that doesn't fit.

1. **[ɜː]** worldwide | urge | fortune | burst
2. **[eɪ]** grape | device | remain | decade
3. **[ʌ]** cultivation | income | sunny | guard
4. **[ɔː]** border | strawberry | boom | shortage
5. **[iː]** seasonal | Latino | leading | remain

6 Word families: Nouns and adjectives

Complete the grid with the correct nouns or adjectives.

Nouns	Adjectives
	wealthy
agriculture	
	short
	attractive
California	
	dry
season	

Station 3: Should we be worried?

wildfire ['waɪldfaɪə]	Flächenbrand
incident ['ɪnsɪdnt]	Vorfall; Ereignis
tanker plane ['tæŋkə ˌpleɪn]	Tankflugzeug
thanks to ['θæŋks tə]	dank; wegen
climate change ['klaɪmət ˌtʃeɪndʒ]	Klimawandel
to **increase** [ɪn'kri:s]	zunehmen; wachsen
to **coordinate** [kəʊ'ɔ:dɪneɪt]	koordinieren
emergency [ɪ'mɜ:dʒnsi]	Notfall; Notlage; Notfall-
flood [flʌd]	Flut; Hochwasser; Überschwemmung
mudslide ['mʌdslaɪd]	Schlammlawine
hillside ['hɪlsaɪd]	Hang
to **collapse** [kə'læps]	kollabieren; zusammenbrechen; einstürzen
to **be willing to do sth** [bi 'wɪlɪŋ tə]	gewillt sein, etw. zu tun; bereit sein, etw. zu tun
to **cut down** [ˌkʌt 'daʊn]	fällen
dehydration [ˌdi:haɪ'dreɪʃn]	Austrocknung
disease [dɪ'zi:z]	Krankheit
bugs *(pl)* [bʌgz]	Ungeziefer
shall [ʃæl]	sollen
to **be to** *(+ inf)* ['bi tə]	sollen
ought to *(+ inf)* ['ɔ:t tə]	sollen
to **be required to** *(+ inf)* [bi rɪ'kwaɪəd tə]	müssen
to **be obliged to** *(+ inf)* [bi‿ə'blaɪdʒd tə]	verpflichtet sein, etw. zu tun; müssen
on average [ɒn‿'ævrɪdʒ]	durchschnittlich; im Durchschnitt
unusual [ʌn'ju:ʒl]	ungewöhnlich
slight [slaɪt]	gering; leicht

crack [kræk]	Riss; Spalt
recorded history [rɪˌkɔ:dɪd ˈhɪstri]	*hier:* Aufzeichnung
all but [ˈɔ:l bʌt]	alle bis auf
indoors [ˌɪnˈdɔ:z]	im Inneren
outdoors [ˌaʊtˈdɔ:z]	im Freien
smell [smel]	Geruch; Duft; Gestank
damage [ˈdæmɪdʒ]	Schaden; Beschädigung
aftershock [ˈɑ:ftəʃɒk]	Nachbeben
conservation [ˌkɒnsəˈveɪʃn]	Schutz; Erhaltung
eating [ˈi:tɪŋ]	Essen; Ess-
smooth [smu:ð]	glatt; weich; geschmeidig
transition [trænˈzɪʃn]	Übergang

7 Find the missing word

Put in the missing words. They are all new in Unit 3.

1. swimmer – swimming pool skater – ______________
2. water – flood mud – ______________
3. interview – interviewee nomination – ______________
4. dry – drought short – ______________
5. poor – poverty rich – ______________
6. to produce – producer to found – ______________

8 What word?

Read the words in the phonetic alphabet and write them down. Use the grid on page 3 for help.

1. [ɪˈmɜːdʒnsi] ______________________
2. [ˈdæmɪdʒ] ______________________
3. [kəˈlæps] ______________________
4. [ˈɪnsɪdnt] ______________________
5. [ʌnˈjuːʒl] ______________________
6. [ˌaʊtdɔːz] ______________________

9 Cause and effect

Complete the sentences with the missing words. The first letters are given to help you.

1. When it's very hot and dry in California, there is a great risk of w______________________.
2. And when there is suddenly a lot of rain after a long dry period, this often leads to f______________________.
3. When people cut down trees, there is nothing to hold the soil, so there are also m______________________.
4. But farmers argue if they let trees die of d______________________, this will cause d______________________ and b______________________ that will then spread to other healthy trees.

10 Opposites

Find the opposite of each word. The words are all new in Unit 3.

1. industry ↔ ______________________
2. nervous ↔ ______________________
3. poverty ↔ ______________________
4. rainy ↔ ______________________
5. outdoors ↔ ______________________

11 Word groups: California

Write the words or phrases in the correct part of the grid.

earthquake | to export | flood | premiere | GDP | minimum wage | wildfire | to boom | animated | bugs | producer | entrepreneur | dehydration | extra | mudslide | Gold Rush | to shoot | nomination

Film	Economy	Environment

Skills: What's important for a handout?

handout ['hændaʊt]	Informationsblatt; Arbeitsblatt
chef [ʃef]	Koch; Küchenchef
training ['treɪnɪŋ]	Ausbildung
substance ['sʌbstns]	Substanz; Gehalt
craft [krɑ:ft]	Handwerk; Gewerbe
deep fryer [ˌdi:p 'fraɪə]	Fritteuse
freezer ['fri:zə]	Tiefkühlschrank

Unit task: My star for the Walk of Fame

selection [sɪ'lekʃn]	Auswahl; Auswahl-
politics *(pl only)* ['pɒlətɪks]	Politik
obstacle ['ɒbstəkl]	Hindernis
to **overcome** [ˌəʊvə'kʌm]	überwinden

Story: Famous

tabloid ['tæblɔɪd]	Boulevardzeitung
to **specialize in** *(AE)* ['speʃlaɪz‿ɪn]	sich spezialisieren auf
to **insist (on)** [ɪn'sɪst‿ɒn]	insistieren; bestehen auf
to **stalk sb** [stɔ:k]	jmdn. stalken; jmdm. nachstellen
to **harass** ['hærəs; hə'ræs]	belästigen; drangsalieren
to **photograph** ['fəʊtəgrɑ:f]	fotografieren
fame [feɪm]	Ruhm
anonymity [ænə'nɪməti]	Anonymität
normality [nɔ:'mæləti]	Normalität

12 Definitions

Put in the missing words.

1. An ______________________________ is a situation, event, etc. that makes it difficult for you to do or achieve something.
2. A ______________________________ newspaper has short articles with lots of pictures and is often thought of as less serious than other newspapers.
3. If you succeed in dealing with a problem, we say you have ______________________________ it.
4. When you are learning the skills that you need to do a job, this is called ______________________________.

13 Odd word out

Cross out the word that doesn't fit.

1. rise | grow | increase | remain
2. drive | stroll | walk | run
3. strawberry | carrot | grape | apple
4. newspaper | magazine | fame | tabloid
5. income | pay | wage | rent

14 Word families

Complete the sentences with a word from the same word family as the word in brackets.

1. Jamie thinks she's a celebrity photographer, not a paparazzo, because she doesn't ______________ (harassment) anyone.
2. I would never give up ______________ (normal) to try my luck in Hollywood; I don't need ______________ (famous) and a lot of money to be happy.
3. Do you really want to go into ______________ (political)? It's not an easy job to do.

15 Check on your ... California words

Make a list of the words that describe California in Unit 3.

____

____

____

____

____

____

____

Text smart 3 Argumentative texts

Tip

Lerne deine Vokabeln immer wieder mal zusammen mit deinen Freunden. So könnt ihr euch gegenseitig abfragen oder auch Tipps geben, wie ihr euch schwierige Wörter am besten merken könnt. Das hilft euch nicht nur beim Vokabellernen, sondern macht auch mehr Spaß!

Introduction

letter to the editor [ˌletə tʊ ðiˬˈedɪtə]	Leserbrief
editor [ˈedɪtə]	Herausgeber/-in; Redakteur/-in
argumentative essay [ɑːgjəˌmentətɪvˬˈeseɪ]	Erörterung
frequent [ˈfriːkwənt]	häufig
to **speak out (about sth)** [ˌspiːkˬˈaʊt]	seine Meinung (über etw.) deutlich vertreten; sich (zu etw.) äußern
insult [ˈɪnsʌlt]	Beleidigung
contestant [kənˈtestnt]	Kandidat/-in
to **break down** [ˌbreɪk ˈdaʊn]	zusammenbrechen
one-sided [ˌwʌnˈsaɪdɪd]	einseitig
to **criticise** [ˈkrɪtɪsaɪz]	kritisieren
to **tolerate** [ˈtɒlreɪt]	tolerieren; dulden

Station 1: How to: Write a letter to the editor

basically [ˈbeɪsɪkli]	eigentlich; grundsätzlich; im Grunde genommen
psychologist [saɪˈkɒlədʒɪst]	Psychologe/Psychologin
My point is … [ˌmaɪ ˈpɔɪntˬɪz]	Was ich sagen will ist, …

host [həʊst]	Gastgeber/-in; Talkmaster
as far as [əz 'fɑːr‿əz]	soweit
to **bet** [bet], **bet** [bet], **bet** [bet]	wetten
to **insult** [ɪn'sʌlt]	beleidigen

Station 2: How to: Write an argumentative essay

to **fail sb** [feɪl]	jmdn. hängenlassen; jmdn. im Stich lassen
sex [seks]	Geschlecht; Sexualität
to **be confronted with** [bi kən'frʌntɪd wɪð]	konfrontiert werden mit
to **present sb with sth** [prɪ'zent wɪð]	jmdm. etw. bieten
sporty ['spɔːti]	sportlich
chest [tʃest]	Busen
muscular ['mʌskjələ]	muskulös
irresponsible [ˌɪrɪ'spɒnsəbl]	unverantwortlich; leichtsinning
exception [ɪk'sepʃn]	Ausnahme
secondly ['sekndli]	zweitens
high-level [ˌhaɪ'levl]	Spitzen-; auf höchster Ebene
to **look up to sb** [ˌlʊk‿'ʌp tə]	zu jmdm. aufschauen; jmdn. bewundern
material [mə'tɪəriəl]	materiell
outdated [ˌaʊt'deɪtɪd]	veraltet; überholt
perfection [pə'fekʃn]	Perfektion; Vollkommenheit
realism ['rɪəlɪzm]	Realismus; Realitätssinn
role model ['rəʊl ˌmɒdl]	Vorbild
to **stop sb from doing sth** ['stɒp frəm]	jmdn. davon abhalten, etw. zu tun

1 Word families

Find a word from the same word family.

1. perfect → ______________________ (noun)
2. criticism → ______________________ (verb)
3. sport → ______________________ (adjective)
4. tolerance → ______________________ (verb)
5. real → ______________________ (noun)
6. insult → ______________________ (verb)
7. except → ______________________ (noun)
8. host → ______________________ (verb)

2 Definitions

Put in the missing words.

1. If you ______________________, you lose control of your feelings and start crying.
2. A ______________________ is a person who takes part in a contest.
3. If you ______________________ somebody, you say or do something that offends this person.

4. A ______________________ is a person that you think is great and you try to copy him or her.

5. ______________________ is a style in literature or art that shows people and things as they are in real life.

3 Check on your ... phrases for presenting your arguments

____

____

____

____

____

____

____

____

____

____

____

____

____

Across cultures 3 Having a voice

Tip

Wenn dich ein Thema besonders interessiert, kannst du auch nach englischsprachigen Podcasts im Internet suchen. Der Vorteil von Podcasts ist, dass du nicht nur mehr über das Thema erfährst, sondern auch authentisches Englisch hörst. So kannst du dir die Aussprache schwieriger Wörter besser einprägen.

to **have a voice** [ˌhæv‿ə ˈvɔɪs]	ein Mitspracherecht haben
participation [pɑːˌtɪsɪˈpeɪʃn]	Mitwirkung; Beteiligung
to **make one's voice heard** [ˌmeɪk wʌnz ˌvɔɪs ˈhɜːd]	sich Gehör verschaffen
student council [ˌstjuːdnt ˈkaʊnsl]	Schülerrat
vote [vəʊt]	Abstimmung; Stimme; Wahl
to **make a difference (to sth)** [ˌmeɪk‿ə ˈdɪfrəns]	etw. verändern
to **admire** [ədˈmaɪə]	bewundern
activist [ˈæktɪvɪst]	Aktivist/-in *(jmd. der sich für etw. engagiert)*
banner [ˈbænə]	Banner; Spruchband; Transparent
to **make one's point** [ˌmeɪk wʌnz ˈpɔɪnt]	seinen Standpunkt deutlich machen
to **believe in sb/sth** [bɪˈliːv‿ɪn]	an jmdn./etw. glauben
petition [pəˈtɪʃn]	Petition; Unterschriftenliste
to **do one's bit** [ˌduː‿wʌnz ˈbɪt]	seinen Teil beitragen
global [ˈgləʊbl]	global; weltweit
protection [prəˈtekʃn]	Schutz
to **spray-paint** [ˈspreɪpeɪnt]	mit Farbe besprühen
fur [fɜː]	Fell; Pelz

coat [kəʊt]	Mantel
to **dictate** [dɪk'teɪt]	diktieren; vorschreiben
belief [bɪ'li:f]	Glaube; Überzeugung
reward [rɪ'wɔ:d]	Belohnung; Preis
to **take the lead** [ˌteɪk ðə 'li:d]	die Führung übernehmen
bubble ['bʌbl]	Blase
bone [bəʊn]	Knochen
valuable ['væljuəbl]	wertvoll
representative [ˌreprɪ'zentətɪv]	Repräsentant/-in; Stellvertreter/-in

1 Collocations

a) *Match the verbs and phrases to make collocations.*

have — do — take — make (3 x)

the lead — one's point — a difference — one's bit — one's voice heard — a voice

1. ____________________ 4. ____________________

2. ____________________ 5. ____________________

3. ____________________ 6. ____________________

b) *Complete the sentences with three of the collocations from a).*

1. We can finish this job on time if we all

____.

2. Keep calm, you needn't shout to

____.

3. If we want this project to work out, we need somebody to

____.

2 Verbs into nouns

Find the nouns that belong to the same word family as the verbs.

1. to protect → ______________________
2. to believe → ______________________
3. to participate → ______________________
4. to vote → ______________________
5. to represent → ______________________

3 Make new words

Use the prefixes or suffixes below to form new words. They are all new in Green Line 5.

im- ir- dis-
un- -istic -ous
-ful -y -al -able

responsible material
trick patient
value comfortable
respectful meaning
adventure logic

1. ______________________
2. ______________________
3. ______________________
4. ______________________
5. ______________________
6. ______________________
7. ______________________
8. ______________________
9. ______________________
10. ______________________

Across cultures 1

1 Word pairs: The world speaks English
human rights, middle class, free elections, ancient culture, racial segregation, plastic surgery, civil rights, surf instructor, square kilometre, sexual harassment

2 A closer look: Three English-speaking countries
South Africa: 1. racial segregation 2. civil rights, elections 3. middle class **India:** 1. Hindu, Muslim 2. ancient 3. democracy, discrimination/sexual harassment **Australia:** 1. Latin, southern 2. Aboriginal 3. crocodiles, lengths

3 Word families: Nouns and adjectives
length, Chinese, democracy, reality, chaotic, racism

Unit 1

1 Safety advice
1. on your own 2. bushwalking 3. netted off, marine stinger 4. snake, disturb 5. rip currents, swept out

2 Odd word out
1. cluster 2. track 3. deadly 4. rip current 5. association

3 Australia: A multicultural country
ancestors, Indigenous, convicts, sentence, oppressed, overseas

4 What word?
1. occupation 2. deliver 3. indigenous 4. farewell

5 Definitions
1. renovate 2. victim 3. Leftovers 4. policy 5. celebration 6. overseas

6 Word search: Aboriginal Australia
↑ territory, elder ↗ tracks, knowledge ↓ guardian → Dreaming ← nomads

1. nomads 2. tracks 3. Dreaming, knowledge

7 What you can do with your face or head
1. to nod 2. to grin 3. to face 4. to frown

8 Nona and me
1. glimpse 2. desk 3. grateful 4. pale 5. conscience
Solution: desperate

9 Opposites
1. ceiling 2. soft 3. previous 4. farewell 5. safety
6. on your own

10 Positive or negative?
Positive: upright, determined, comforting, enthusiastic, soft
Negative: desperate, awkward, disrespectful

11 Phrasal verbs
a) call off, show around, trace back, stand up for, be involved in, glance at
b) 1. show – around 2. trace – back 3. called off
4. was involved in

12 Synonyms
1. on one's own 2. no longer 3. litter 4. soil 5. celebration
6. overseas

13 Check on your ... Australia words
snake, air ambulance, bushwalking, box jellyfish / marine stinger, rip current, barbie, ancestor, convict, Dreaming, elder, to trace back, indigenous

Text smart 1

1 Word families
1. emotion 2. understanding 3. to introduce

2 Alicia's Hollywood story
fate, annoyed, misery, supporting role, hysterical

3 Check on your ... film words
clip, crew, appearance, cast, supporting role, wide shot, visual, onlooker

Unit 2

1 Word search: Job applications

← employer, attachment ↑ weakness, applicant ↘ interview
↓ gender ↗ reference

1. applicants, interview 2. weaknesses 3. gender
4. References

2 Word pairs: It's all about jobs

1. c) 2. e) 3. f) 4. a) 5. b) 6. d)

3 Say it in a different way

1. Furthermore 2. at all times 3. profession
4. opportunity, required

4 Odd sound out

1. require 2. gender 3. consider 4. firefighter

5 Word families

1. focused, responsibility 2. associate 3. Hopefully
4. signature 5. adventurous

6 Nouns into verbs

1. to involve 2. to volunteer 3. to harvest 4. to plant

7 What word?

1. exhausted 2. volunteer 3. controversy 4. religious

8 The cocoa controversy

provides, cocoa, cosmetics, poverty line, forces, plantations, chop, pods, machetes, physically, beans, dump

9 Definitions

1. tricky 2. toothbrush 3. colleague 4. laws

10 Odd word out

1. employer 2. applicant 3. machete 4. commitment
5. common

11 Guess the right verb

1. matter 2. acknowledge, selected 3. standardized
4. make a choice 5. dare

12 Verbs into nouns

1. ability 2. assignment 3. laugh / laughter 4. apology

13 Positive or negative?

Positive: satisfied, hard-working, fulfilling, patient, focused, meaningful

Negative: exhausted, selfish, impatient

14 Opposites

1. hard-working 2. patient 3. rarely 4. female 5. the elderly 6. weakness

15 Check on your ... job words

testimonial, qualification, applicant, position, responsibility, CV, application letter, gender, employer, all-rounder, weakness, profession, organiser, people skills, reference, (job) interview, pay, wage, to be a team player

Text smart 2

1 Definitions

1. currently 2. earthquake 3. review 4. journalist 5. outcome 6. recruit

2 Find the missing word

1. researcher 2. performance 3. fall 4. to conclude

3 Check on your ... summary phrases

In an article posted on / published in ..., the author states ... / mentions ... / argues ... / points out ... / ...; According to the writer, ...; The author's main point is ...; The writer goes on to say ...; The author also believes that ...; The author illustrates ... by ...; The writer concludes by stating ... / pointing out ... / asking ... / using ... / ...

Across cultures 2

1 Word families

1. acceptable 2. to free 3. horrible 4. tolerance 5. problematic

2 Tolerance and respect
1. prejudice 2. provoke 3. offend 4. mainstream 5. privacy
Solution: diversity

3 Phrasal verbs
a) be prejudiced against, slow down, go by, stand out, be passionate about, fit in, bring up, come out
b) stand out, fit in, come out, prejudiced against, passionate about

Unit 3

1 Word friends
1. b) 2. e) 3. a) 4. f) 5. d) 6. c)

2 Hollywood Dream Factory
aspiring, luck, premieres, glitz and glamor, effort, pursue, cattle calls, showcase their talent, keep their head above water, agent

3 A mind map: Describing people in a positive way
Individuelle Lösungen.

4 California's economy
1. Golden 2. shortage 3. silicon 4. drought 5. income 6. dot-com
Solution: worldwide

5 Odd sound out
1. fortune 2. device 3. guard 4. boom 5. remain

6 Word families: Nouns and adjectives
wealth, agricultural, shortage, attraction, Californian, drought, seasonal

7 Find the missing word
1. skatepark 2. mudslide 3. nominee 4. shortage 5. wealth / fortune 6. founder

8 What word?
1. emergency 2. damage 3. collapse 4. incident 5. unusual 6. outdoors

9 Cause and effect

1. wildfires 2. floods 3. mudslides 4. dehydration, diseases, bugs

10 Opposites

1. agriculture 2. relaxed 3. wealth 4. sunny 5. indoors

11 Word groups: California

Film: premiere, animated, producer, extra, to shoot, nomination
Economy: to export, GDP, minimum wage, to boom, entrepreneuer, Gold Rush
Environment: earthquake, flood, wildfire, bugs, dehydration, mudslide

12 Definitions

1. obstacle 2. tabloid 3. overcome 4. training

13 Odd word out

1. remain 2. drive 3. carrot 4. fame 5. rent

14 Word families

1. harass 2. normality, fame 3. politics

15 Check on your ... California words

glitz and glamor, cattle call, wannabe, premiere, extra, agent, founder, producer, wealth, Gold Rush, start-up company, dot-com bubble, agriculture, fortune, shortage, drought, Hispanic, silicon, device, entrepreneur, wildfire, flood, mudslide, fame, to showcase one's talent, to shoot, to boom, to export, aspiring, backstage, animated, golden, sunny

Text smart 3

1 Word families

1. perfection 2. to criticise 3. sporty 4. to tolerate
5. realism / reality 6. to insult 7. exception 8. to host

2 Definitions

1. break down 2. contestant 3. insult 4. role model
5. Realism

3 Check on your ... phrases for presenting your arguments

In my opinion, ...; As far as I know, ...; I am convinced that ...; Because of ...; My point is that ...; The fact / truth is that ...; It is obvious that ...; Although ...; Some might say that ...; Don't let anyone tell you that ...; It is a typical mistake to say / think / claim ...

Across cultures 3

1 Collocations

a) have a voice, do one's bit, take the lead, make one's point, make a difference, make one's voice heard

b) 1. do our bit 2. make your point / make your voice heard 3. take the lead

2 Verbs into nouns

1. protection 2. belief 3. participation 4. vote 5. representative

3 Make new words

impatient, irresponsible, disrespectful, uncomfortable, materialistic, adventurous, meaningful, tricky, logical, valuable

Bildquellennachweis
U1.1 Alamy stock photo (Vadym Drobot), Abingdon, Oxon; **U1.2** Getty Images RF (E+/narvikk), München; **2.1** shutterstock (shurkin_son), New York, NY; **7.1** Dream Maker Software (RF), Colorado; **7.2** Thinkstock (Hemera), München; **8.1** Thinkstock (esancai), München; **13.1** Adobe Stock (Monkey Business), Dublin; **35.1** laif (Daniel Rosenthal), Köln; **44.1** shutterstock (goodluz), New York, NY; **53.1** shutterstock (Vic Labadie), New York, NY; **56.1** shutterstock (Ekaterina Pokrovsky), New York, NY

Sollte es in einem Einzelfall nicht gelungen sein, den korrekten Rechteinhaber ausfindig zu machen, so werden berechtigte Ansprüche selbstverständlich im Rahmen der üblichen Regelungen abgegolten.